SOPHIA'S NEW MOTHER

MAIL ORDER BRIDES OF FORT RIGGINS

SUSANNAH CALLOWAY

Tica House
Publishing

Sweet Romance that Delights and Enchants!

PERSONAL WORD FROM THE AUTHOR

Dearest Readers,

Thank you so much for choosing one of my books. I am proud to be a part of the team of writers at Tica House Publishing who work joyfully to bring you stories of hope, faith, courage, and love. Your kind words and loving readership are deeply appreciated.

I would like to personally invite you to sign up for updates and to become part of our **Exclusive Reader Club**—it's completely Free to join! We'd love to welcome you!

Much love,

Susannah Calloway

VISIT HERE to Join our Reader's Club and to Receive Tica House Updates!

https://wesrom.subscribemenow.com/

CONTENTS

CHAPTER 1

Heat waves shimmered in the afternoon sun, turning the golden stretches of the southern fields into a half-dreamt mirage. Curtis Emerson paused for a moment to catch his breath beneath the spreading oak that provided the only shade for three acres. He took his hat off and dropped it to the cool ground, then followed it, heedless of the dirt. The sparse grass there in the welcome relief of the shade was still alive and growing – struggling, there was no doubt about it, but at least it was still pale green as opposed to the wheat-colored heads of the prairie grasses that covered most of his property.

Wiping sweat from his brow, he leaned against the trunk of the oak and surveyed the job at hand. Two horse corrals, a smaller and a larger, separated by a split-wood fence. That crazy storm that came through the week before had brought with it scores of jagged lightning – not to mention an anxiety headache at the worry over fires being started all across the county. The lightning had struck the tallest corner post and rendered it – well, it had been split-wood to begin with, and now it was little more than kindling. Toothpicks. He was fortunate that the brief flare of flame in the age-hardened wood hadn't lasted long enough to spread to the dry grass outside the bare dirt of the corral.

Curtis lifted his head to look up into the wide-set branches of the old oak.

"How on earth did you survive that storm?" he muttered to it. "Sheer doggedness, I reckon. You been here a lot longer than I have – and you'll still be here when I'm gone." He rubbed his hands together, returning his gaze to the job in front of him. "Outlive all of us, I'll bet," he said. "Last forever." He sighed. "But nothing lasts forever."

As they often did, his thoughts drifted back to the day, now ten years ago, when he had looked up from his work in the fields to see his mother-in-law rushing toward him, skirts in one hand, waving at him wildly with the other. Even before she'd come close enough for him to hear, he'd known something terrible had happened...

Sometimes, he found himself wishing he could go back to that moment before Louise came close enough for him to make out her words. Things were so much simpler, then. He still had a wife, Sophia still had a mother, Louise still had a daughter. They'd been the perfect happy little family.

His reverie was interrupted by a familiar voice.

"Hey there, boss. Looks like you're taking today off, eh?"

Curtis came back to himself with an effort and gave his foreman a smile.

"You should have seen me five minutes ago, Andy. I was sweating like a pig."

"You mean you've just been sitting here for a whole five minutes? You're setting us a bad example, boss." Andy sat down beside Curtis, stretching out his legs in front of him and giving a sigh of contentment. "On second thought, I can see why. A fellow could get used to this."

"Maybe you ought to tell the hands to take an hour or two in the afternoon, Andy, and go inside. Just during the hottest part."

Andy made a doubtful face.

"Don't know if they'll like that. Hard enough to make a living without taking time away from work."

"I won't pay 'em any different. I'd rather they get paid for sitting in the bunk house for an hour rather than collapse in the heat and get laid up in bed for days. It's hot as blazes out here – far hotter than it was last year in June. No creature should be out in the sun when it's like this."

"No creature indeed," Andy agreed. "Man or beast. That's what I came to tell you – we just finished putting up the fence in the north quarter, and I've set the boys to rounding up the herds and moving them through."

Curtis sat up a bit straighter.

"That's good news. I wondered if that might get done this week. Say, Andy, that's quick work – it's only Tuesday, and I hadn't counted on it being done until Friday or Saturday."

"The boys were motivated to work fast," Andy said, waving a hand dismissively. "To get out of the sun, I reckon."

Curtis grinned at him.

"Well, whatever the reason, I'm glad to hear it. That north quarter's got more trees than the rest of the acreage put together. The herds'll be much happier in there."

"There's still quite a bit of grass that hasn't withered, too, so we can cut down on their feed for the next few weeks, like as not."

"Good, good." Curtis rubbed his chin thoughtfully. "I hate to look at the ledgers for longer than a minute for fear they'll give me a headache. But that will help." He gestured to the corral. "And if I can get this fence repaired, we can get back to training. That'll help, too."

"I don't envy you, trying to run this place on your own," Andy said candidly, rubbing the back of his neck. "The most rest you ever get is spare moments like this when it's either sit down or fall down. I'm happy enough just to be a foreman. Figuring out expenses and whatnot – well, numbers are not my cup of tea."

"Not mine either, to be honest with you," Curtis said. "But I do what I've got to, just like any man would. Besides, I'm not doing this completely on my own. Louise and Sophia help out wherever they can. And I've got you and the other hands." He reached out to clap his foreman on the back. "Somehow, we'll muddle through another hard summer."

"Sure," said Andy, starting to stand up. "Just in time to muddle through another hard winter. Say, Curt, the boys and I are heading into town to go to the saloon tonight. We'd be honored if you'd join us."

Curtis got to his feet, dusting himself off.

"I'd like to say yes," he said. "Seem's like a coon's age since I've been to the saloon. Maria still working there?"

"She was the last time I was in."

"So, last week then."

Andy chuckled, his expression a little abashed, and Curtis laughed.

"Remember me to her, will you? She went to school with my – with Ruth. Came to our wedding. Always asks after Sophia whenever I see her in town."

"Sure, boss. I reckon that means you ain't coming with us?"

Curtis shook his head.

"Not tonight," he said. "It's Sophia's birthday. Can't miss out on supper with her – if my calculations are correct, there'll be cake."

"How old is she now, Curt?"

"Just turned thirteen."

Andy shook his head.

"Seems like just yesterday she was chasing after us and telling us to be kinder to the farm dogs. Do you know that girl used to throw dirt clods at us when she thought we weren't being nice enough to the animals?"

Curtis shook his head, caught halfway between chagrin and amusement. "She's got her ma's fiery personality, that's for certain," he said. "Stubborn as all get out, too. But the most caring person I've ever had the privilege to meet, all the same."

"That come from her ma, too?"

"Must have," said Curtis, turning toward the waiting corrals. "She sure didn't get it from me."

Andy shrugged. "Oh, I don't know, boss," he said. "In the seven years I've known you, I've come to believe that you're a man of hidden depths." He grinned at Curtis and waved as he turned to go. "Maybe really *well* hidden, but there all the same."

"Go on with you, lay-about, get back to work – and enjoy the saloon."

Shaking his head and smiling ruefully, Curtis steeled himself to head back out into the sun and finish the job ahead of him.

CHAPTER 2

"Sophia. Where did you go?"

Sophia glanced over her shoulder as her grandmother came into the sitting room. Worry had etched a permanent line between her brows, but when she saw the girl standing at the window, her face relaxed just slightly.

"I turn around and you disappear. I've finished frosting the cake – thought you might like to lick the spoon." Louise Brown put a hand on her granddaughter's shoulder and leaned past her to squint out the window. "What are you up to in here?"

"Just watching for Pa," Sophia said. She folded her arms, patting absently at her grandmother's hand on her shoulder. "He said he'd come in early tonight so as to make sure he was home for supper, but I don't reckon that he will."

"Why ever not, Sophia? Your father is generally thought of as a man of his word."

"Sure," said the man of his word's daughter, "but only if you don't try to get between him and his work." She sighed. "He ought to have come in for the afternoon. It was blistering hot out there."

"And you were up in the hayloft," said Louise knowingly. "It's nearly as hot up there as it is out in the meadows."

Sophia gave a little shrug.

"I just wanted to think about things, that's all," she said. "I'm thirteen now, Grandma – that's practically grown up, isn't it?"

Louise smiled at her fondly and stroked her long brown braid.

"Sometimes it seems like it," she said. "When I look at you and see how tall you're getting – and you look more and more like your mother every day. Why, you're the spitting image of her when she was your age."

Sophia nodded slightly, her eyes fixed on the yard outside the window, waiting for the slightest hint that her father was coming.

"I know it," she said. "That photograph Pa keeps in his bedside table – I take it out and look at it sometimes when he's working." She hesitated for a moment, chewing on her lower lip. The next words seemed to burst forth from her. "I wish Ma hadn't died, Grandma. I know you and Pa are doing your best to raise me right, but – well, some things a girl just wants a mother for."

Louise was quiet for a moment, still stroking Sophia's hair. She slipped her arm around the girl and hugged her.

"I know," she said. "I understand, dear – and I miss your mother, too."

Sophia glanced swiftly at her grandmother, alerted by the tremulous tone in her voice, and saw the beginning of tears in her eyes. Quickly she turned to face her and threw her arms around the older woman.

"I didn't mean to make you cry, Grandma – I know Ma was your only daughter, and you must miss her as much as I do."

"Yes – yes, of course, I do. But in a different way, dear. Mothers and daughters…" She sighed, put her hands on Sophia's shoulders, and looked her in the eyes. "There's something special about that, something truly precious. And of course, I got to see my little girl grow up, fall in love, marry and have a little one of her own." She cupped Sophia's chin and smiled, despite the tears that still stood in her eyes. "When I see you, it's almost as though I've got her back again. And you were so young when we lost Ruth…"

Sophia nodded, fighting back a wave of her own emotion.

"Yes," she said, putting a hand to her forehead and glancing back at the window as though she couldn't help herself. "I can't really remember her much – but I know what it must be like to have a mother. All the girls at school talk about their ma's – and I end up feeling left out." She shook her head a little. "I'm worried about Pa, too. He's going to keel over from exhaustion, the way he's going. Is it because we don't have enough money? Is that it?"

"I don't think a girl your age needs to be concerned about things like that, Sophia."

"Why not?" Sophia asked candidly. "In three or four years, I'll be old enough to get married if I want to. I'll have to know about these things. Besides, if Pa would just let me, I know that I could help him with more."

"You do very well at your chores," her grandmother told her, patting her on the shoulder again. "You do all that is asked of you, and never complain. Well..." She smiled. "Very rarely, anyhow."

"But I could do more," Sophia said, her face setting into a stubbornness that was very familiar to Louise – and which she seemed to have inherited from both parents. "If he would just let me..."

"He doesn't want you to have to grow up too fast, that's all, Sophia."

Sophia folded her arms again.

"Then maybe he should get someone else to help him. I'm sure Andy wouldn't mind."

"Andy's the foreman, dear. He doesn't do the books. He's not trained, and to be honest with you, as flighty as that young man can be, I would hesitate to trust him with the ranch's accounts."

"Someone else then," said Sophia, with determination. "Maybe he could get Annie at the inn."

"Annie works quite enough as it is. I doubt she'd want to take on any more."

"Well, maybe..." Sophia said, and stopped suddenly as an idea occurred to her. Her eyes suddenly became very bright, and she turned to her grandmother slowly. "Grandma, do you think that it would do Pa any good to get married again?"

Louise shot her a sharp-eyed glance, but Sophia only looked back at her innocently.

"Why do you say that?"

"Well, it's been ten years," Sophia pointed out practically. "And I think we would all agree that he needs help with running the ranch. And maybe if he gets married again, he won't work himself into an early grave. And besides..." She dropped her gaze to the floor. "Besides, then I could have a mother again."

Louise sighed deeply and put a hand on Sophia's arm.

"I understand how you feel," she said. "And no, it wouldn't be a bad idea – but I don't think your pa will every marry again."

"Why not?"

"Well, dear, just think of it. We know every young woman in this town. Who would you see your father getting married to?"

Sophia was quiet for a moment, mulling it over. As much as she hated to admit it, her grandmother was right.

"Maybe a girl from somewhere else, then," she said. "Grandma, what about writing to a matrimonial agency? My friend Clara said that her cousin Byron married a girl from New York City, because he put an advertisement in one of the big papers, and she answered it. Clara says they're happy as could be."

But Louise was already shaking her head.

"No, dear – I'm quite certain your father would never agree to such a thing. And when it comes to stubbornness, he can give you a run for your money." Another sigh, another pat, and Louise turned to head back out into the hallway, kitchen-bound. "Come along and help me with supper, dear. I'm sure your father will be in any moment."

For a few minutes more, Sophia watched out the window. She had spoken honestly, candidly to her grandmother – she worried deeply about her father. He poured every waking moment, his whole heart and soul, into the ranch. She knew it was for good reason – he wanted to care for what was left of his family, after all. No one could fault him for that. He was a good man.

Still, she couldn't help but wish he was a little bit more of a father, rather than merely a ranch owner.

Sometimes it seemed they had grown apart more and more every year. She knew he didn't understand her; perhaps that was only to be expected, as he was a thirty-six year old man and she a thirteen-year-old girl. But shouldn't he try, even so?

She couldn't remember the last time he had given her more than a perfunctory embrace, or had any real warmth in his smile, or sought out her company at anything more than breakfast or supper. He was physically present in the home, but his mind was acres away, working out the newest conundrum or mentally parsing the ledgers that covered the surface of his desk in the study. Yes, he had given his heart and soul to the ranch and had none left for his daughter.

If he married again, fell in love again, maybe he would reclaim that heart and soul, find someone worthwhile of caring for them...

At last, just as she heard her grandmother call plaintively for her from the kitchen, she saw her father approaching through the golden sunlight of the early summer evening.

Supper was a plentiful affair. It usually was, of course, but Louise had taken pains to ensure that this was a meal to be remembered.

"After all," she said, smiling at Sophia as she set the main course on the table, "how often does my only granddaughter turn thirteen?"

"Only once," said Sophia, laughing. "Unless I get it wrong – maybe I'll get another chance."

She glanced over at her father to see if he was appreciative of her silly joke, but he was frowning thoughtfully into the distance.

"Pa?"

"Mm – yes, Sophia?"

Sophia took the plate her grandmother handed her. In obvious surprise, her father glanced down at the plate that had appeared in front of him.

"What are you thinking about?"

"Mm, well – to be honest, I was thinking about the hands. They're all headed into the saloon tonight."

"Oh," said Sophia, a bit deflated. She sat back in her chair and put her fork down. "Would – would you rather go with them?"

Curtis Emerson took a bite of the shepherd's pie his mother-in-law was famous for. He chewed for a moment, eyeing his daughter. Then he swallowed and grinned.

"Wouldn't miss this for the world," he said. "After all, how often does my only daughter turn thirteen?"

There was more warmth in his voice than she had heard for a long time. She responded to it, smiling back and sitting forward again. She picked up her fork.

"No, I was only wondering what sort of shape they'll be in tomorrow. We're moving the cattle into the north quarter, and we'll have to stockpile some hay and grain in the shed over there. The grass is better there than just about anywhere else, but it won't hold them forever. Jack Payne is coming next week to survey the ones he's picked out, and I'm half afraid he's going to try and convince me I tagged 'em wrong, but I know those critters like the back of my hand…"

Once her father got started ruminating on business, it was almost impossible to get him to stop. As he spoke with increasingly more depth and passion about the herds, the warmth Sophia had felt began to ebb away. Yes, he was capable of mustering up some interest and affection for her – but how much he lavished on the animals that he cared for. Wasn't that a bit backwards?

19

It was becoming ever more clear to her that her father needed to learn a lesson – a lesson in how to love his fellow humans, and not just the ranch.

She felt the final surge of conviction after they'd had their cake, and the presents were brought out. First was a neatly wrapped little package from Louise, who handed it over to her granddaughter with a kiss on the forehead and a warm smile. Sophia unwrapped it and gave a little cry.

"Paints and charcoal. Oh, Grandma, how did you know?"

"If you think I haven't noticed how you come back from the hayloft with ink on your fingers, then you've got another think coming," Louise told her, smiling broadly. "You've got a talent for drawing, Sophia – I'm sure you'll have the same knack for painting, as soon as you get the chance." She turned to Curtis. "Just like her mother did – don't you remember how Ruth would do those little paintings for her friends, when she was young?"

"I do," said Curtis, but his tone was rather crisp. Sophia eyed him; she couldn't tell whether he was disapproving of his mother-in-law's gift, or whether he was simply distracted by his own thoughts. Perhaps it was a mixture of both. She set aside the sadness this gave her and instead concentrated on smiling brightly at her grandmother.

"Thank you, Grandma," she said simply, and hoped her voice would tell her grandmother how deeply she appreciated the gift.

Louise knew her granddaughter well.

The two of them, almost without realizing it, turned to look at Curtis. He looked between the two of them and then offered a rather sheepish grin.

"It's all right, Pa," said Sophia quickly. "I'm just glad you're here, that's all."

"Aww, you don't think I forgot about your birthday present, do you?" He dug in his pocket. "I thought, what does a thirteen-year-old girl really want? And I couldn't come up with an answer. So here." He pressed a few coins into her hand, the sheepishness of his smile not abating even as he did so. "Don't spend it all at once, Soph."

Sophia looked down at the money in her hand.

"A whole dollar," she said softly. "Why – thank you, Pa."

He must have picked up on the tone in her voice, for he shifted uncomfortably.

"I just wasn't sure what to get you," he said, a little stiffly. "But this way you'll have plenty of money to pick out what you really want." He glanced over at his mother-in-law as though for reassurance that he had done the right thing, but she was looking at Sophia and would not meet his gaze. "Get something you really need, Soph," he said again. "Don't spend it on something, I don't know – silly. Get something practical, something you'll really use – something with some real value."

21

Sophia glanced down at the little paint set and charcoals that had taken the place of her cake plate. "You mean – not like that?"

Curtis sighed heavily.

"Now, you know I don't mean anything of the sort," he said. "All I mean is – well, you know best. It's your dollar. Spend it how you like." He stood up from the table, squinting out the window. "There's still a good hour of daylight left. I'm going to finish up the corrals so I can start on the north shed tomorrow. Thank you for supper, Louise."

He hesitated, and then brushed a kiss on the top of his daughter's head. Sophia did not dare look up until he left.

Louise reached over to take her plate, beginning to clear up the table.

"You know he didn't mean anything by it, dear," she said. "Your father loves you more than anything else in life."

Sophia did not reply. Her mind was in a whirl. *Buy something practical, Sophia. Something with real value. Something you really need.*

A dollar would easily purchase an advertisement in one of the big newspapers in the east. Maybe two or three, if she was careful with it. And she could write the advertisement herself, she knew she could. It would be easy. All she had to do was tell the world that her father was a handsome widower who owned a ranch, and that he was badly in need of the love of a good woman. He'd have women knocking down his door.

Louise, looking into the dining room from the kitchen and saw the sudden firming of her granddaughter's lips, and knew what it meant. It meant Sophia had made a decision. It meant she was about to spring into action and wasn't about to let anything get in her way.

Above all, she knew, it meant trouble.

CHAPTER 3

The heat of summer had descended on Boston like a blanket, cloaking the respectable old city in a smothering welter of irritation and brightly-lit gloom. Far off on the horizon, nearly hidden behind the tall buildings that lined the streets, a storm was beginning to build. But the promise of rain was still a distant hope. From three stories above, Edie Kendall saw passers-by moving slowly, turning their heads upward now and then to peer anxiously for any sign of relief from the sheer might of the sun.

By contrast, her father's study was cool and dark, the shades drawn at eight o'clock each morning in order to preserve what freshness had been brought by the night before. Despite the contrast, she couldn't help but envy her fellow city-dwellers down there on the street. None of them were waiting to be given bad news.

Her father, as though drawn by the thought, entered the room at last. Edie stepped back from the window, twitching the curtains into place to block out the sun. She blinked in the sudden darkness; it would take her eyes a moment to adjust, she knew. In the meantime, she made her way by familiarity to the seat across from the desk and waited until her father gestured toward it before sitting. He was a dim shadow in the gloom.

"Well, I'm sure you must have anticipated what I'm to tell you," he said without making any attempt at pleasantries. "I've just come from a business meeting with Mr. Crowell, and we have reached an agreement."

He tapped his fingers on the desk, practically beaming with pride in himself. "The two of you are to marry next month – or, if proper arrangements can be made, sooner. Now, Edyth, Mr. Crowell is a very important man, and he will expect you to do your duty as his wife without making a fuss. You'll host dinners and parties and – " He waved a hand dismissively, as though none of it were really worth discussing. "See to the children, things like that. Above all, he expects you to be a pillar and a support." He eyed Edie, his bushy gray brows drawing down over his nose. "As do I."

Watching her father, Edie's heart sank. His words were correct – she had anticipated this. But preparation for the news did not make it any more palatable or easier to accept. For the last several months, she had seen her father begin to do his best to ingratiate himself with Mr. Crowell, a man who was his superior in fortune and his contemporary in age. Burton Crowell's first wife had passed away from a heart complaint late the year before; Gordon Kendall had seen in this "job opening" an opportunity to promote his daughter and, not coincidentally, himself. Nearly every week since the beginning of spring, Mr. Crowell had joined them for dinner. He wasn't a bad-looking man, even if he was a year older than her father. No, if his age was the only objection to him, she would go along with her father's plan without a word of complaint.

It was what she knew about Mr. Crowell's business tactics – his lack of scruples and ethics, the deplorable conditions under which his factory workers labored, the families that he had ruthlessly turned out of the tiny flats he rented out for more than market price – that had turned her against him. Neither did she appreciate how he had started to size her up with his eyes, as though he viewed her as an acquisition to be made – one which may or may not have been worth the price. Evidently, her father's persuasion had made its mark at last.

Well, he might scheme all he liked. The fact was that he couldn't do anything unless Edie agreed – and the more she thought about it, the less inclined she was to do so.

She took in a deep breath.

"Father, I don't want to marry Mr. Crowell."

There was a pause as her words sank in. Somehow, though she wouldn't have believed it possible, her father's brows drew down even further over his nose as his keen-eyed stare turned steadily into an outright glare.

"I beg your pardon, Edyth?"

Edie straightened up, squaring her shoulders.

"I don't want to marry Mr. Crowell," she said. "And that's that."

Perhaps the "that's that" was going a bit too far, she realized, as her father stood up from his desk.

"Is that so, missy? Is that so? Well, you just listen to me. Mr. Crowell has been so kind as to not only offer to provide for you for the rest of your life – presuming that you're acceptable to him as a wife – but also to give me a partnership in his business concerns. Just think of that, will you, before you go turning up your nose at such a generous offer. He's going to make not only you a wealthy woman, but your father a wealthy man."

Edie clasped her hands together in her lap, trying to keep them from shaking. She didn't like confrontation at the best of times, and in her twenty years of life, she'd done her best to avoid them. Especially had she done so in the past four years, since her mother had passed away. Oh, if only Mother were here now. She would never let her husband put his foot down like this, never let him promise their only child in marriage to a man like Burton Crowell.

But she wasn't there to protect Edie. The only person Edie could rely on was herself.

Slowly, she stood, wishing she was taller to confront her father on more equal grounds. She lifted her chin.

"I'm sorry that your business proposition won't worked out as planned," she said. "Perhaps Mr. Crowell will understand if you tell him my feelings on the matter."

"Oh? And just what are your feelings?"

"I have no wish to marry a man like Mr. Crowell. He may be well respected in the business community, but I have no respect for him personally. When I marry, it will be because I've chosen the man, not because someone else has forced me into it."

Her father's eyes were so wide she could see the whites ringing the dark irises.

"You listen to me, daughter," he said. "I raised you to obey your elders and betters, and I'm not about to back down from that lesson now. As long as you are under my roof, you'll do as I say. And as soon as you're married and gone, you'll do as he says. Don't go fooling yourself into thinking there will ever be a time when your choice will come first – unless I or your husband chooses to allow it. There's not another word to be spoken on the subject. The arrangements are made, and that's the end of the matter." He sat down again, waving a hand at her, and turned his anger to the pile of papers on his desk. "That's all. You are dismissed."

For a moment, Edie hesitated. It certainly didn't seem to her there was no more to be said, nor did it seem the end of the matter. She had plenty more to say about it. But her father was quietly grinding his teeth, and she knew that if she continued, it would only make things worse.

How could they be worse? she lamented to herself silently. Only if he grabbed her by the ear and marched her out to marry Mr. Burton Crowell that very minute. And with the temper he had, she wouldn't put it past him.

Clenching her jaw, she turned and left the study. She closed the door cautiously, careful not to slam it for fear this would further engage his ire, and then sped swiftly down the hallway to the room at the end, which housed the library. It wasn't a large library, especially not compared to the fine libraries in the houses of some of her friends. But every wall was lined with books, and there was always a stack of newspapers and periodicals on the table that she read voraciously, to keep up her knowledge of the goings-on in the outside world. The outside world, far away from her little gilded cage in Boston...

How could her father be so...so...so ignorant and unfeeling as to put his pursuit of wealth above the happiness of his only daughter? It wasn't as though they were deprived of anything; they had always had a well-stocked pantry, at least two servants, and she'd never lacked for new clothing. What more did her father want? Why was he so driven by greed – so driven by his desire for more, and more, and more?

She sat down and put her elbows on the table, looking down and thinking hard. No matter what her father said, no matter what he threatened, the fact still remained that she was twenty years old, and he could no more force her to marry Burton Crowell than he could force her to join a convent. And she would not do either just to please him.

She had her own ideas of what a marriage should be like – she always had. While her mother had been alive, she had seen how a man and wife could argue and disagree…and yet still maintain their love for each other. As difficult as her father was, there was no doubt that her mother had loved him deeply, though she had been forced to stand up to his schemes and demands on a regular basis. And he had loved her, as well – she vividly remembered him grumbling when his wife disagreed with him, but he almost always capitulated. But now that she was gone…

She sighed and rubbed a hand across her face. She missed her mother dearly, and the fact that her father had turned into a tyrant after her passing only made it all the worse. But there was nothing to be done about it. As he had said, she lived under his roof, and would be expected to follow his rules.

But did that really give him the right to dictate the rest of her life?

She simply could not fathom it.

Seeking a distraction from the turmoil in her mind, she picked up the latest copy of the Boston Times that sat on the top of the stack of periodicals. For the next several minutes, she paged through the closely typed articles, doing her best to occupy her mind with the news of the city and nation. But it seemed no use. Her father's words, his stern tone, his angry glare were always there at the back of her mind.

She turned to the last page of the paper. Here there were advertisements – people seeking out long-lost relatives or friends, a woman who had misplaced her spectacles on a park bench last week, a governess looking for a new position. Edie brightened for a moment; perhaps she could find employment. Surely someone, somewhere must want a companion or something along those lines. But the only advertisements appeared to be those of individuals looking for work, rather than employers looking for employees. Her mood lagged once more; after all, she told herself realistically, it was unlikely she would be able to get a job when she had no real skills or experience. She couldn't be a teacher, and she had no inclination to be a governess. No, if she was going to take care of children, then they would be her own.

Sighing deeply, she let her eyes wander through the scant remainder of the advertisements on the page. A few words caught her gaze, and she sat up straight, giving the advertisement her full attention.

The wording was simple and straight to the point. It painted a picture of a widower, a man of thirty-six years, who owned a ranch in a place called Fort Riggins, Montana. He was looking for a helper on the ranch – but more importantly, a wife for himself, a mother for his daughter.

Edie took in a breath and held it for a moment, reading over it again swiftly. She'd heard of things like this – she'd even seen a paper called the Matrimonial Times, which seemed dedicated to bringing together lonely hearts. But the last place she expected to see such an advertisement was on the back page of the Boston Times. Did this poor man not know about matrimonial agencies and such things? Whatever the case, her pity was stirred – and so was her interest.

She sat back in her chair, staring into space as her thoughts picked up speed. If her father was insistent that she obey his commands and dictates while she lived under his roof, then perhaps the only option was to move away. He certainly couldn't expect her to bow to his every whim and decision if she was living elsewhere – and especially not if she was a married woman.

The best detail was that Fort Riggins, Montana, sounded a very long ways away from Boston, Massachusetts.

No, she didn't know this man, this – she scrutinized the advertisement once more – this Curtis Emerson. But he sounded honest and straightforward enough, which was more than could be said for Burton Crowell. And she was quite willing to learn how to help manage a ranch, along with a family.

She had enough savings tucked away to purchase a train ticket – and first, of course, to send a telegram.

Would she go? Could she really do this, leave her home and only surviving family behind?

Before she had even fully formulated the question, she knew the answer. She could – and she would. Her father was determined to decide her future on her behalf, with no regard for what she wanted. If she was to escape his plans for her, she must act quickly and take her future into her own hands.

She couldn't afford to wait even a day longer. She must leave that very night – as soon as she could catch a train heading west to the great unknown.

She could only pray that her decision was the right one.

CHAPTER 4

Two weeks after her thirteenth birthday, on the first of July, Sophia Emerson came walking slowly home from town. She meandered up the drive, opened the little picket fence and picked her way through as carefully as though walking on eggshells, taking care to close it behind her, and then poked along to the veranda. There she stopped and stood for a moment, looking up at the front door as though expecting some inspiration. None came; she took a deep breath and started up the steps, her manner growing more and more urgent as she went. By the time she burst into the kitchen she was practically running.

"Grandma?"

"Oh, there you are, Sophia. I'd wondered where you'd got to." Louise Brown looked up with her usual half-glad, half-worried smile, then looked back down at the pot she was stirring almost immediately, evidently not perceiving the expression of bemusement on her granddaughter's face. "Did the general store have the baking powder, or are those shelves still as bare as they were the other day? I've told Matt Garner a dozen times that he needs to order more stock each month, but he's pretty set in his ways…" She looked up again, this time seeing the pensive look on Sophia's face. "They didn't have it, eh?"

"Well…" Sophia brought her hands forward. She clasped an envelope. Nervously, she shifted her weight side to side. "To be honest, Grandma, I plumb forgot to go to the store."

"You forgot?" Louise raised an eyebrow. "That's the whole reason you walked into town, you silly goose."

"All right, maybe I didn't forget, exactly," Sophia hedged. "Only – well, I went to the post office first, and there was a letter for Pa. I had to come home and talk to you about it."

"If it's a letter for your pa, what on earth have you and I to talk about? Goodness, Sophia, you'll be the death of me." She put the spoon down on the spoon rest and turned to her, folding her arms. "Now, what's going on?"

"Well, there's a little bit of a story to it," Sophia said, still stepping side to side nervously. "Remember on my birthday how we talked about whether Pa should get married again…"

35

"Yes, indeed." Louise tutted. "It wasn't a conversation that I'm likely to forget. We should just be grateful that your father wasn't there for it."

"Well – he's going to have to be for the next one."

"What on earth do you mean?" Louise eyed her sharply. Sophia grinned sheepishly at her.

"You remember that he gave me a dollar for my birthday…"

"I reckon I do," said Louise, turning away to face the pot again, her lips thinning into a firm line. She hadn't been entirely approving of her son-in-law's gift; Sophia was quite sure that her grandmother felt it showed a lack of interest. Her feelings on the subject were not that dissimilar from Sophia's.

"And he told me to use it for something valuable – something I really needed."

"Child, stop drawing this out or we'll both die of old age before you get to the point. What did you do?"

Excitement humming around the edges of her words, Sophia said, "I wrote for Pa a Mail Order Bride."

If she had wanted to shock her grandmother, she got her wish. Louise's eyes opened so wide that Sophia was half afraid they would fall right out of her skull.

"You did *what?*"

"I wrote a letter and sent it out to some of the biggest papers in the east," Sophia said. "George at the post office helped me figure out which ones. He was very helpful, really," she said, full of half-malicious glee at being able to share this with her grandmother. George was Louise's second-cousin's son, one of the few family members left in Fort Riggins, and Louise had a tendency to believe he could do no wrong.

Louise put a hand to her forehead. "Oh, child – you never did."

Sophia nodded.

"It's done." She shrugged. "I really believed it was the right thing to do, Grandma – I still believe it. Only...now I'm thinking about what Pa will say when he finds out..."

"Goodness, he'll have a fit." Louise twined her fingers together anxiously. "Well, go back to that scoundrel George and tell him that he's got to help you put it to rights. You can write back and cancel the advertisement. I'll give you money for the postage if you haven't got it..."

"Grandma, Grandma – it's too late." She held out the letter, her hand shaking just a little. "This is the reply. It's a telegram, and the newspaper sent it on with a note. Her name is Edyth Kendall – and she'll be here in three days."

If Louise's eyes had seemed wide when the news was first broken to her, it was nothing compared to the expression of shock that she bore now.

"Sophia Anne Emerson."

"That's why I had to tell you, Grandma," Sophia said, a pleading note entering her voice. Things never went well when her grandmother started using her full name. "You've got to help me figure out how to tell Pa."

"Tell Pa what?"

Both Louise and Sophia froze, staring at each other. There was no mistaking Curtis's voice; there was no mistaking that he was coming down the hallway toward the kitchen, either. There was no time to debate what to say or when – the time was now.

Sophia turned to face her father, who was now standing in the doorway, looking on both of them with a puzzled frown.

"Well, Pa..."

She cast a frantic glance over her shoulder at her grandmother. Louise cleared her throat.

"It seems that Sophia has been worried about you," she said. "And out of love and concern..."

"That's right. Out of love and concern..."

"...she wrote to see about the possibility of a Mail Order Bride for you."

Curtis raised his eyebrows. For the moment, he didn't seem to be as enraged as Sophia and Louise had feared. He bore an expression of mild bemusement, more than anything. Perhaps he was still thinking about the tasks waiting for him outside. Sophia leapt in.

"What are you doing here, Pa?"

"Well, goodness, Sophia, can't a man enter his own kitchen without his daughter asking questions like that?"

He moved past her and went to the stove top, inhaling deeply from the steam coming from the pot. "I spilled half the water from my flask. I was headed around the house to the pump when I heard the two of you chattering away and got curious. Can't stay long, we're in the middle of putting up the lean-to in the north meadow," he said to Louise. "That smells good. I'll wait for supper." He turned back to Sophia and folded his arms. "Now, what's all this about a Mail Order Bride?"

As Sophia had thought, he'd been distracted by his work. But now he seemed to have finally registered the words, and his expression was more keenly interested. She swallowed hard past the sudden lump in her throat, her nerves threatening to get the best of her.

"I wrote an advertisement for a wife and mother," she said. "Someone that can help out with the ranch, too. I sent it to some of the biggest newspapers back East, and they ran it last week."

Curtis sighed and pinched the bridge of his nose between his fingers.

"I think I feel a headache comin' on," he said. "And it's got your name all over it, Soph. What on earth possessed you to – no, never mind. Don't bother trying to explain it, I can't imagine that I'll ever understand. Just...just write and cancel it."

"That's what I said," said Louise. "But..."

Curtis turned to his mother-in-law.

"But?"

"But it's too late," said Sophia. "She's on her way."

"Who is?"

"Edyth Kendall. Your new wife."

Curtis stared at his daughter. The realization of what she was telling him seemed to crash over him slowly, and the expression of bemusement turned to shock and then, more quickly, to anger.

"You're tryin' to tell me," he said slowly, "that you went behind my back and made arrangements for a woman to come out here – telling her she can expect to marry me?"

Sophia squirmed under the fire in his gaze.

"Yes..." she said, her voice quite small. She only just caught the look of sympathy that her grandmother cast her.

Curtis took in a deep breath and let it out again, obviously trying to control his anger.

"Well, Lord," he muttered. "Sophia, you know better than that. I raised you better. Your ma would be crying into her pillow over hearing you do a dumb thing like that. Write to this poor fool and tell her not to come."

"I can't, Pa – she's already on the way."

"Then you go and meet her at the station and tell her to head on back where she came from."

"Pa."

"No," he said sharply, holding up a hand to stop her. "I don't want to hear another word. I didn't ask this woman to come here, and I'm sorry she got caught up in your foolish actions. You're responsible for her, Sophia. I don't want anything to do with it. You broke it – you're going to fix it."

He turned on his heel and stormed out of the kitchen and down the hallway. After a moment, they heard the front door slam as he made his way angrily back to his work. Sophia stood silent for a moment, and then Louise came to her and put her arms around her.

"I'm sorry, dear – he's right, it was a foolish thing to do. But I'm sorry he was so angry."

"I reckon he has a right to be," Sophia said, shivering a little. "Still – I wish he would just listen to me sometimes. Hear me out." She turned a teary-eyed gaze to her grandmother. "He never listens to what I have to say."

"He's a man, dear. They're not equipped."

"He's my pa. You'd think he would at least try."

Louise sighed and stroked Sophia's hair.

"There's one thing he's wrong about," she said. "He told you that your ma would cry over what you did. But I knew my daughter better than he did, though they were husband and wife."

Sophia's face took on a tinge of hope, and Louise smiled at her.

"She wouldn't have cried. She would have laughed so hard that she fell over."

Louise hugged Sophia tighter as the girl laughed despite herself, holding her all the more tightly as the laughter turned into tears.

CHAPTER 5

There seemed to be no adequate word for the exhaustion that Edie Kendall felt as the train rolled finally into the small town of Fort Riggins, Montana. *"Tired"* certainly did not cover it. *"Wretched"* was a bit closer. She stretched her arms and yawned as the train puffed to a stop, trying to wake herself up a bit. It had been several sleepless nights and uncomfortable days – if she never got on a train again, she thought, it would be too soon.

Along with the exhaustion, her nerves were playing up as she looked out the window at her new hometown. Throughout the journey west, she had spent most of the time daydreaming about what her new life might be like – and, most especially, what the man she was going to marry might be like. She knew he couldn't possibly be as bad as Burton Crowell; that was the main thing. But he was undoubtedly an imperfect man, just like every other, and she knew it would be unwise to expect too much.

All the same, she couldn't help but indulge in a little speculation – and a little hope along with it.

She pictured him as tall, broad-shouldered, and handsome. He must be strong, as he was a rancher. He was a good bit older than she, so perhaps he had gray hair beginning at the temples, giving him a distinguished air. She knew from experience that it was far more likely he was beginning to lose his hair entirely, but that knowledge didn't quite fit in with the romantic daydreams with which she occupied her time during the train travel, and so she decided to pretend she'd never seen a bald man in her life.

Well, the moment of truth had arrived, just as she had arrived in Fort Riggins. She was about to step off the train, and he would approach her any moment now...

Clutching her valise so tightly that her knuckles turned white, she stepped off the train and held her breath, daring to look around.

There was...no one.

Well, not precisely no one, she corrected herself. She wasn't the only passenger disembarking at Fort Riggins, evidently. Two cars up from where she stood, a mother and her young son were busily gathering their packages and baggage and hugging the middle-aged man who had come to greet them.

Nearer to her, a studious-looking fellow with his hands in his pockets was striding away from the train, evidently knowing precisely where to go even without anyone there to greet him. The crowd on the platform was rather sparse other than that, she had to admit; in fact, it couldn't rightly be called a crowd at all.

No matter where she looked, a tall, broad-shouldered, handsome rancher with distinguished gray at the temples failed to appear.

There was, however, a young girl and an older woman standing at the edge of the platform. Was Curtis Emerson, perhaps, standing behind them? She craned her neck to see, and as she did so, the two looked at each other and then hurried forward.

The girl looked to be about twelve or thirteen. She was tall and slim, with brown hair pulled back in a thick, neat braid. She twisted her fingers together in apparent nervousness, but stood forward and spoke first, nonetheless.

"Miss Edyth Kendall?"

Edie blinked at her. The girl was nearly as tall as she was herself and seemed to be quite self-possessed. Edie wondered whether perhaps she was older than she'd thought.

"Yes," she said, "I am Edyth Kendall. Er – whom do I have the pleasure of speaking to?"

The girl's pretty face relaxed into a smile.

"I'm Sophia," she said, holding out a hand for a shake. "Sophia Emerson. And this is my grandmother Louise."

Realization dawned on Edie, and she gave a short sigh of relief.

"Ah, I see. You must be Mr. Emerson's daughter. Goodness, I'm so pleased to meet you." She dropped her bag and took the girl's hand eagerly, then couldn't keep herself from throwing her arms around her in a swift embrace. Sophia Emerson straightened her back briefly in surprise at this unexpected gesture, but just as quickly relaxed into the embrace and returned it warmly. Edie stepped back and reached for the grandmother's hand to clasp it as well, smiling at the older woman. "For a moment there I thought he hadn't come to meet me at all."

"Er…" Sophia and her grandmother exchanged a glance, and then Sophia turned back to Edie. "Well – he didn't, actually."

Edie looked beyond the girl's shoulders. Indeed, there was no one waiting at the entrance to the platform, no one bashfully anticipating his introduction to his bride-to-be.

"Oh," she said, unable to hide her disappointment. "Well – I suppose he was otherwise occupied. Your father must be a very busy man, running a ranch all by his lonesome. I don't know much about it, to be honest," she confided in the girl, "but I'm really quite looking forward to learning. No doubt he's out with the – with the cattle." She gave a little shrug and managed a smile. "And sent the two of you to collect me, since he couldn't be here himself."

Another swift look between grandmother and granddaughter, and Louise cleared her throat.

"That's right," she said, and smiled at Edie. "You're our responsibility from here on out – isn't that right, Sophia?"

Sophia bent and picked up Edie's bag, standing up straight and tall again with a brave smile.

"Right," she said. "And now – let's go home. And then…then we can talk."

There was some underlying meaning to her words that Edie didn't quite understand. But there on the platform hardly seemed the place to ask for an explanation. At least she hadn't been left there in the dying sun of the summer twilight, expected to fend for herself. And the two seemed quite personable and friendly, even if they were a little on the mysterious side.

Willingly enough, she followed them as they set out for the street. She couldn't help but wonder, as they stepped out into the little town of Fort Riggins, what might lie ahead.

CHAPTER 6

Her curiosity was not laid to rest right away. This was a challenge for Edie, who knew that impatience was among her major faults, but she resolved to let her new friends choose their own time for speaking. So, as they loaded her valise into the little farm cart that waited on the street outside the train platform, and as they made their slow way out of town, she listened to Sophia Emerson chatter about the sights of Fort Riggins without asking any questions about their rather odd behavior – or about why, precisely, Curtis Emerson did not meet her himself.

She had to own up to the feeling of disappointment that weighed rather heavily on her shoulders. Though she'd only hatched this plan just over a week ago, still she had spent a great deal of time picturing the moment they would meet. There had been no doubt that it would occur on the platform, just after she arrived. But as she thought about it, she brightened up a little. Now, the first meeting would certainly occur tonight, in the ranch house. He would welcome her to his home, take her hand and give her a long, meaningful gaze with warmth and humor in his eyes, tell her how sorry he was to have missed collecting her and how glad he was that she had arrived at her new home at last...

Yes, surely it would be something like that. And, after all, his being tall, broad-shouldered, handsome, and distinguished didn't depend upon the location of their first meeting. He could be all of those things just as easily in his own house as he could on the train platform.

With that thought in mind, she was able to pay more attention to what Sophia was telling her about the town. There really didn't seem to be much of it – an inn, a saloon, the mercantile, a feed store, a few other bits and pieces – but she listened and nodded and smiled. Sophia gave a bashful smile as Louise drove the horse and cart out of town at last.

"I reckon it's not much, compared to Boston," Sophia said. "What's it like, living in a big city like that?"

Edie shook her head and sighed.

"It's loud...busy...there's no getting away from people." She glanced off to the side. With a single turn in the track, the sights and sounds of town had rapidly faded into the distance, and they were suddenly surrounded by a quiet stretch of golden-headed grasses, with purple mountains in the distance.

"You're right, Sophia, it is very different in comparison. But from what I've seen of your Fort Riggins so far..." Edie paused for a moment, listening to the sound of peaceful silence, and smiled. "I can't say but that living here in Montana might be a leap forward for me."

Sophia beamed at her.

"I hope so," she said. "I'd be so pleased if you like it here..."

Her grandmother gave her a slight nudge with her elbow and a wordless murmur, and Sophia sighed.

"Well – I do hope so, anyhow."

She lapsed into silence for a few moments. Edie was avidly curious about what that little exchange meant precisely, but she decided to hold her tongue and wait.

She was glad that she did, for around another bend was the entrance to the Emerson Ranch. She couldn't help but catch her breath at the picturesque beauty of it: a wide, still pond with the track winding around it, leading past a small stand of oaks to the long, low ranch house, neatly whit-washed and tidily kept. Behind it was a stand of outbuildings, including an enormous structure she assumed must be the barn. Two smaller areas were fenced in, with a post in the middle of each.

In the distance, beyond the house and outbuildings, spread a vista of golden grass, dotted with a few far-off trees. The lavender twilight was settling in, and a peaceful breeze stirred the grasses, rippling them into waves.

"I've never seen anything quite like this," Edie managed. She clasped her hands in her lap. Sophia reached over and touched them.

"Welcome to our home," she said happily.

In short order, Louise and Sophia bundled Edie out of the cart, led her up the stairs of the veranda, and conducted her inside. She had scarcely a chance to take in her surroundings – neat, clean, and tidy, as she would have expected – before she had been installed in an overstuffed chair in the sitting room. The window was open, and a cool breeze blew through the room. Sophia took a seat near her, and Louise went to the door.

"I expect you're starving," she said. "I'll fix you a plate." She gave her granddaughter a meaningful glance and then disappeared down the hallway, shutting the door after her.

The time had come, Edie felt, for explanations.

"I'm absolutely overcome with curiosity at this point," she said, turning to the younger girl. "I feel as though there's something going on here that I don't quite know about. Will you tell me, whatever it is?"

Sophia sighed.

"I reckon I'd better," she said. "That's why Grandma left us alone for a little while – I wanted her to stand by me, but she made it pretty clear that I was the one who ought to tell you…"

"Tell me what?" Edie leaned forward in her chair. Sophia avoided meeting her gaze, and Edie reached out to take the girl's hand. "Don't worry," she said softly. "I won't be upset. Just please – tell me. What's wrong?"

Sophia squirmed a little in her chair.

"I think you might be upset," she said. "And it won't be your fault if you are – it'll be mine. See, there's a reason why Pa didn't come to meet you at the train station. And the reason has to do with what I did."

"Yes? And what is it that you did?"

"I wrote a letter," said Sophia.

"A letter?"

Sophia nodded and wiped at her nose with the back of her hand. Edie pulled a handkerchief from her pocket and passed it to the girl.

"Now, now, don't cry. Just tell me. What letter?"

Sophia took in a deep breath, hunching her shoulders over.

"I wrote a letter to the Boston Times," she said, "and to other papers to – to put in an advertisement for my father."

Edie stared at the girl blankly. Sophia looked up, and something that she saw in Edie's expression made her hurry into an explanation.

"He didn't know anything about it, you see. I thought it would be best for him to get married again. My mother's been gone for ten years – I barely even remember her. And Pa's a good man, only he – well, he works too much. And he's not happy. I just wanted him to be happy…"

"Are you telling me," said Edie slowly, "that you're the one who wrote the advertisement that I answered in the Times – on your father's behalf?"

Sophia nodded, looking miserable.

"And he never intended to marry again?"

"No – he says he doesn't want to."

Edie felt panic begin to overtake her. She stood and began to pace, pressing her hand against her forehead.

"I think I feel a headache coming on…" she muttered.

"Oh, that's what Pa always says when he's angry with me." Sophia sprang up, twisting her hands together. "Don't be angry with me, Miss Kendall, please."

With an effort, Edie managed to control herself. It was on the tip of her tongue to speak harshly to the girl, to question why on earth she would do such a thing. She was certainly old enough to know better. Perhaps that was the trouble –

she was of the age where ideas could be both formed and acted upon. And though they had not known each other long, Edie could tell Sophia was a clever girl, and clearly determined. Stubbornness, she suspected, was an integral part of her nature.

She couldn't help but feel some sympathy with that.

She came back to her seat and sat down, taking in a series of long, slow breaths to try and calm her racing heart.

"I am not angry with you, Sophia," she said. "I am – concerned, surely." *Concerned?* Like *exhausted*, the descriptor didn't even begin to cover how she felt. "If your father didn't place the advertisement and has no intention of being married, you must understand that it leaves me in rather a predicament."

"I know, I know... but I had hoped he would change his mind," Sophia burst out. "And he might. He might still. Once he sees you – you're so pretty and kind, he won't be able to refuse to get to know you. Why, anyone would want to."

"That's very sweet of you," said Edie with a rather testy sigh, "but I'm afraid that it's also rather foolish. Your father is a grown man who can make decisions of his own..."

"Not very good ones," Sophia observed frankly.

"And that's quite a disrespectful way to speak of him."

"You don't even know him, Miss Kendall."

"I may not know him, but I know very well how a daughter should and should not speak to her father." She knew all too well, in fact – hadn't she had similar run-ins, expressed similar thoughts, about her own father? Again, she felt a dart of sympathy for the girl seated by her. She sighed. "It can certainly be difficult, of course, to speak respectfully when he does or says something that you don't agree with. But you're still a child, Sophia, and living under his roof. You must do your best to understand and support his decisions."

Sophia nodded, though it was with obvious reluctance.

"I reckon you're right," she said slowly. Then, hesitantly, she added, "I wish he could see what a good mother you would make."

Edie looked at her oddly. The statement was certainly an unusual one to make, and she was on the verge of asking what on earth Sophia meant by that when the door opened, and the man of her dreams stepped in.

Tall, yes. Broad-shouldered, yes. Handsome – yes, yes, and yes.

Good Lord, he even had the beginnings of gray dusting the temples of his otherwise dark hair. Faint, to be sure, but there, nonetheless.

Edie's mouth went dry.

The only thing that kept him from being entirely made from the stuff of daydreams was the fact that his dark eyes went to her immediately – and just as immediately narrowed as though he were...suspicious of her, somehow. Suspicious... or angry...

He stopped cold in the doorway, so swiftly he rocked back on his heels.

"I do apologize," he said stiffly. "I didn't realize this room was occupied."

Then, in the space of a blink, he was gone. She heard a heavy tread going down the hall and up the stairs. A moment later, the faint sound of a door closing in what was not quite, but almost, a slam.

She turned wide eyes on Sophia, who sighed.

"Well," said the girl, "I reckon you've finally met Pa, at last."

CHAPTER 7

The next few days were rather a whirl for Edie Kendall.

True, the ranch itself was quiet and peaceful, far more so than anywhere else she had ever been. But Sophia Emerson was a bit of a spitfire. She was extremely self-possessed for a girl her age, and also extremely busy. She helped her grandmother with running the household with a clockwork precision, and her duties evidently extended to milking the cows and maintaining the garden. On the first day, Edie followed her around to try and help, and by the end of it, she was absolutely exhausted.

"I don't know how you manage all of this," she confessed at the end of the second day. "And so young."

They sat in the kitchen, Louise standing at the stove. Sophia took a sip of her tea and smiled at Edie.

"Grandma taught me everything I know," she said.

"I don't know about that," Louise said with a delicate snort. "I reckon you know a few things I never taught you – and I can't imagine where you picked them up."

Sophia laughed and Edie chuckled.

"Perhaps she inherited them," she said. "Some things are just in the bloodline, you know."

"Goodness, what a terrible thought," said Louise, and they laughed again. Sophia took another sip of her tea and stood up hastily.

"I forgot. Clarabelle's brooding in the oak outside the hen house – I'd better go and check on her."

She skipped out through the open kitchen door, and Louise took a seat at the table across from Edie, shaking her head and smiling.

"She really is something else, that girl," Edie observed.

"She keeps us on our toes, that's for certain."

"She's very sweet, though – I like her a great deal."

"I'm glad to hear it," Louise said softly. "She likes you, too." She turned the mug of tea between her hands. "I don't suppose you've given more thought to what you might do?"

Edie sighed.

"I know I should," she said. "I suppose over the last few days I've just been trying to avoid it. I'm so very tired after the journey here."

"Of course, you are. There's no rush, my dear. My only concern is for your welfare."

"I appreciate that, Louise. The truth is…" She shook her head. "The truth is, I can't simply go back home to Boston. I left under – rather troublesome circumstances." As briefly as possible, avoiding details wherever she could, she explained what those troublesome circumstances were. Louise listened with an expression of deep sympathy on her face and shook her head and tutted once Edie finished the tale.

"Goodness, my dear – I certainly understand. Well, as I said, there's no rush at all. You're welcome to stay here with us while you figure out what you'd like to do. We'd be honored to have you."

"Mm." Edie sipped her tea. "I don't think that your son-in-law would feel the same way. It seems he's managed to avoid me entirely since that first night. I hate to think I'm making him uncomfortable in his own home."

Louise opened her mouth, closed it again, and then tried once more.

"Curtis is…a good man. He's just stubborn. Set in his ways. Something that he certainly passed down to his daughter." She smiled fondly. "He's a bit awkward about all of this, it's true, but if you need to stay longer, he'll come around. He's very kind, really. And of course, Sophia would be delighted if you chose to stay longer – or even if you decided to stay in Fort Riggins for good."

As much as she was drawn to the peaceful, country surroundings of Fort Riggins, the idea of staying in the town all by her lonesome was not immediately appealing to Edie. She shook her head and decided to leave that possibility for later thought.

Instead, she said, "What do you suppose possessed Sophia to put in the advertisement to begin with? Goodness, it's clear she's a bright girl, and I assume she must have known how her father would react. I suppose any man would react much the same, really."

Louise lapsed into a pensive silence, staring into the depths of her tea without seeming to see what was in front of her.

"Hope makes us do things," she said at last. "Things that we might not do, otherwise. Sophia lost her mother when she was very young, scarcely two years old. As she grows older, she and her father grow farther and farther apart. He doesn't quite know what to do with her, a young woman who could run rings around him if she chose. He does his best, I'm sure, but – well, perhaps he could show her a little more care, a little more understanding."

She sighed. "As foolish as it was for her to write that advertisement, I understand what moved her to do so. She's already lost her mother. She's afraid she'll lose her father, too." She looked up and her eyes met Edie's directly, honestly. "She hoped that a new wife would be a good influence on him, as well as a helper. She hoped she would gain a mother, as well, something so vital, so precious, that she's been lacking most of her life. I cannot blame her for what she did – I only wish it hadn't been at your expense."

Edie nodded, dropping her head to break their shared gaze. Louise's pain was obvious and intense – after all, it wasn't just that Sophia had lost her mother, and Curtis Emerson his wife. Louise had lost her daughter, as well. It struck Edie hard, the realization that a woman who filled so many roles must of course have a deep and wide-spread impact on all those around her who had relied on her. After all, hadn't she felt it when her own mother had passed away? And she knew her father had felt the loss keenly, too.

"I understand it," she said softly. "My mother passed away unexpectedly about four years ago – I know how Sophia must feel. It's a terrible thing."

"But of course, you did not try to arrange a marriage for your father," Louise said.

"No." Edie laughed gently. "Quite the opposite. I had just turned sixteen, and I did my best to take over my mother's role in the household. I made sure my father had everything he needed, from his favorite shirts always being pressed and clean to his dinner always being on time. I suppose I wanted to make sure that he knew he had not lost everything, though my mother was gone."

She thought for a moment, then shook her head. "He did not respond well – that is, he did not respond as I would have hoped. We had always been somewhat at loggerheads, and my mother had stood up for me. Without her there, and with me trying to reassure him and avoid conflict, he simply became more and more of a tyrant as the days went by. I so desperately wanted him to know that he had not lost me, I never quite realized that I had lost him long before – or, perhaps, that I never had him at all."

In the silence that stretched on after she stopped speaking, Louise reached over and put a hand on hers. Her eyes were bright with unshed tears of sympathy.

"It seems we have all suffered a great loss," she said. "Perhaps that's the real reason behind our meeting. To comfort each other – to remind each other to hope."

Hope – if only it were easier to keep in mind. But despite Louise's kind words, despite Sophia's obvious adoration, Edie could not help but think of that cold, bitter expression on Curtis Emerson's handsome face, the one time she had seen him. He had already made his decision, that much was clear. And if he would not even meet with them for meals, what chance did she have to change his mind?

No, despite Louise's words, her situation was...hopeless.

CHAPTER 8

Clarabelle the brooding hen was doing perfectly fine, thank you very much, and needed no help from any inquisitive human girl. She gave a low, warning cluck as Sophia approached.

"All right, all right," Sophia placated her, holding up her hands. "I only wanted to make sure you had what you needed, after all. What sort of hostess would I be, otherwise? Not a very good one at all."

Leaving a container of water and a small pile of grain within easy reaching distance, Sophia turned and headed back to the kitchen. As she approached, the sound of voices drifted out. It was Edie's voice she heard first.

"What do you suppose possessed Sophia to put in the advertisement to begin with?"

The conversation carried on, and Sophia froze. She knew she shouldn't, but she was desperate to listen. Suppose they said something important, something that they would never say in front of her. But there was a word for this – eavesdropping. And both her father and her grandmother had told her off more than once for the habit. Well, she didn't mind being told off once more – but suppose Edie found out she was listening? Why, she would be so disappointed.

Feeling simultaneously virtuous and regretful, Sophia left the intriguing conversation behind and went around to the other side of the house. Now, she could come in through the front door, making noise and loudly announcing she had returned. Or she could leave them to it for a while – perhaps they needed to have a discussion, after all. She could go to the hayloft and draw for a little while, practice with her paints until it was closer to time for supper...

Despite her intentions, she continued on past the barn and found herself rounding it to reach the lone pine that stood a little way off from everything else. It was a peaceful area, the grass around it kept trim and neat by her father's efforts. At the base of the old pine, nestled between two thick outspreading roots that humped out of the ground like embracing arms, was the small stone marker.

Sophia sat down beside it with a sigh.

"I reckon it's been a few days since I was here," she said. "It's been...well, it's been busy."

She reached out to trace the name carved on the marker, peeling away the small patch of moss that had grown since she was last there.

"Sorry, Ma," she said contritely. "I ought to do better, I know. Well." Sitting cross-legged, her skirts over her knees, she leaned an elbow on her knee, and her chin on her fist. She thought for a little while, pensively.

"I did it," she said. "What I told you I was going to do. And now she's here – her name is Edyth Kendall, but she said to call her Edie. Not even Miss Edie – just Edie. Like we were already friends." She was quiet for a moment, and her smile slowly faded. "I don't know how long she'll stay, though, Ma – I don't think my plan worked at all."

Suddenly, the emotion of the past few days – perhaps of the past few years – overwhelmed her and she buried her face in her hands, her shoulders shaking as she sobbed. There seemed to be nothing in the world beyond her grief – and then suddenly there was something more, something solid, something comforting. Familiar arms were around her, pulling her in, and her father was patting her on the back, his tone half worried, half bewildered as he said her name over and over.

"Sophia – Sophia – what is it, Soph? What is it?"

The unexpectedness of his presence, let alone the note of love in his voice, was too much to bear. Sophia abandoned herself to weeping for the moment, almost enjoying it – simply because her father was there with her, doing his level best to comfort her.

After a few long moments, however, she pulled herself together and sat up straight. Her father was on his knees in the grass beside her, his eyes full of anguished concern. A bouquet of late spring wildflowers, nearly blown from the heat, was abandoned at his side. She'd almost forgotten that he had a habit of bringing flowers to her mother's grave every week – it had been a few weeks since she'd been there herself, and so she hadn't found them. But of course, he wouldn't forget. He wouldn't neglect the memory of the past...

She wiped her eyes with the back of her hand. Curtis fumbled in his pocket for a handkerchief and handed it over. Sophia wiped her eyes and sniffled.

"What are you doing here? I thought you were still working on the north field."

He gave her a slightly exasperated sigh.

"One of these days, I hope to show up somewhere on my own property and not have someone ask me that. What are you doing here, if it comes to that? I take a short respite from work to take a peaceful little walk and find my daughter sobbing in the dirt. Scared me half to death."

"Sorry, Pa," Sophia said, though only reluctantly. "I came out to talk to Ma for a while – but I just got thinkin' about things, and…"

Curtis saw the tears nearly starting again and hastened to comfort her.

"There, there, child – don't cry anymore." He put an arm around her. "Why don't you just tell me what's going on?"

Sophia couldn't remember the last time that her father had asked her to explain how she felt. It was enough to bring on the tears again, despite his frantic attempts to calm her.

"I'm sorry I meddled in your life," she wailed, flinging her arms around him. "I really didn't mean to – I mean, I reckon I meant to, but – only because I thought it was for the best. I don't want you to be unhappy, Pa – and I miss Ma – I know I never really knew her, but I miss her anyhow. I thought Edie would make both of us happy – but instead I've just made you angry and her upset, and I'm downright miserable." She buried her head in her father's shoulder. "What can I do to fix it, Pa?"

Curtis drew a long breath and tightened his arms around his only daughter. They sat in silence for a long few moments before he finally spoke.

"Maybe there is no fixing it," he said at last. "Maybe the only way out is through. Soph, there's no doubt that you made a mistake – but there's also no doubt that you only meant the best by it. I can't hold that against you."

"Then what do we do? I don't want to carry on like this, Pa – Edie's going to go back to Boston, I'm sure of it, and things will just go back to the way things were. But I'm afraid..." She gathered her thoughts, feeling driven to absolute, utter honesty, no matter what her father might say or think. "I'm afraid we won't have each other anymore. We don't ever talk like this – and I want to. I... I miss you, Pa."

She couldn't mistake the stricken look on her father's face as he stared at her. He swallowed hard and smoothed a wayward lock of hair out of her face.

"Well," he said, and had to stop and clear his throat. His voice suddenly sounded very husky, almost as though he were fighting off tears of his own. "We can't have that, can we? All right, Sophia. If you think Miss Kendall will be such a big help to you, then I'll do my best to give her a fair shake. I won't promise anything – I've no intention of getting married again, and I can't pretend otherwise. But I also can't stand to see my little girl in tears when there's something I might do to make her happy again." He put a finger under her chin and lifted it until she was looking at him. "Will that make you happy, Sophia? If I agree to try and get to know Miss Kendall?"

"Yes," Sophia breathed. "Yes, it'll make me very happy, Pa – so very happy."

She flung her arms around him, and he heaved a sigh.

"Very well, then," he said. "I'll be friendly to Miss Kendall, and you promise to accept the outcome, whatever it may be. She may very well decide to go back to Boston – and nobody would blame her. But we'll cross that bridge when we come to it. Do we have a deal?"

Sophia nodded eagerly. "Deal."

"Shake," her father prompted, holding out a hand. She did so, a grin spreading over her face that mirrored his own. It was a wonder, she thought, how quickly tears could turn to smiles – when everyone took the time to just talk about things.

And now, her father would have the chance to see how wonderful Edie was – and he couldn't help but fall in love with her and ask her to marry him.

She was almost certain of it.

Her plan was coming together nicely after all.

CHAPTER 9

Surprised wasn't the word for how Edie Kendall felt when Curtis Emerson joined them for supper that night. In fact, it didn't even begin to cover it. What would? She wasn't sure. Perhaps there wasn't an accurate way of putting it, after all; *surprised* might just have to do, in a pinch.

So – she was surprised.

First of all, by his very presence – and, as a quick second, by the fact that he took his seat at the head of the table, flashed a smile at everyone else, and then turned to Edie herself.

"I guess we haven't been properly introduced," he said.

"Er…" She shot a glance at Sophia, who was grinning ear to ear. "Yes – I suppose that's true."

"And it's my fault," Curtis Emerson said frankly. He held a hand out to her for a handshake. Disarmed by his honest and rather blunt approach, she took it. "Please, call me Curtis," he continued.

"I – thank you. Yes. Um." She bit her lip. How was it that he could make her so frazzled with just a simple smile and a few words? "Edyth Kendall. I'm pleased to meet you at last."

His hand was warm and rough.

"Do you have everything you need, Miss Kendall?"

"Please call me Edie. Yes, of course, Sophia and Louise have been very thoughtful."

He grinned.

"Not like me," he said. "Puttin' me to shame, in fact. Well, I'm glad to hear it." He turned to Louise and gave her a smile. "I'm sorry I've missed supper these last few nights, Lou."

"That's all right, Curtis." Edie could tell by the expression on Louise's face that she was just as baffled as Edie was herself – and just as pleased, too. She dished up a plate for Curtis first, then Edie and Sophia and herself. "I figured you've been awfully busy with moving the cattle."

"That's so, I have been," he said agreeably. "Still, that's no excuse for being rude to our guest, let alone to you and Sophia. I'll do my best to be on better behavior from now on."

Louise gave him a smile, though she still looked rather confused by this sudden change of heart.

"Is there a lot to be done on the ranch at this time of year?" Edie asked.

"There's always a lot to be done," Curtis said, nodding. "Seems like just about every time I think I've got it all handled, something else picks up, and I'm back where I started. Louise and Soph are tremendous helpers, of course."

Edie smiled at Sophia, who was fairly glowing with pride at her father's words.

"Well, I don't know much about life on a ranch," she said. "I don't really know anything, to be honest – but I'm happy to help. While I'm here."

Curtis met her gaze. His eyes seemed to search into hers with an inquisitive force she could feel all the way down to her toes. At last, he nodded, and his face relaxed into a smile once more.

"I appreciate that," he said. "And I'll take you up on it. We can always use another set of hands around here."

It wasn't much, but it was certainly something. She couldn't put a name to it, but she knew how it made her feel – triumphant, as though she had won a challenge. As though she'd taken the first big step in the right direction.

Though it seemed nearly impossible, the stuff of dreams, perhaps there was hope for her and Curtis after all.

Over the next few days, they began to settle into an easy routine. Edie spent most of the day with Sophia and Louise, helping to cook and clean and mend. Sophia would disappear now and then, but when Edie asked about where she was going off to, Louise just smiled and shook her head.

"She's got her little hobbies," she said. "I'm sure she'll show you when she's ready."

In the long evening twilight, after supper and before the sun was entirely down, they sat together in the sitting room. After that first supper they enjoyed together, Curtis approached Edie with a ledger in his hands.

"Did you mean what you said about helping out with the ranch?"

She blinked up at him.

"Of course. I meant every word."

He nodded, giving her a grin.

"How are you with mathematics?"

After that, an hour was spent every evening in his study, going over the books together. Evidently, Curtis had gotten rather behind through the busy season. Though numbers were certainly not Edie's cup of tea, she remembered enough of her schooling to pick up the basics quickly, and the time that was needed to cipher everything grew shorter and shorter. By the time her first week at the ranch had passed, they needed only twenty minutes to finally catch up and bring the ledger up to date. Curtis thumped the heavy book closed with a sigh and leaned back in his chair.

"Thank you, Edie," he said. "I needed a second pair of eyes to go through it with me. I might never have caught that discrepancy on my own. All I knew was that the numbers weren't adding up."

"You're quite welcome. It's the least I can do after the generosity that your family has shown me."

He eyed her speculatively.

"Now that the books are all caught up," he said, "they'll only need updating every week or so, just to keep 'em maintained. I don't suppose you'd like to take on that job? It would be a big help to me."

"Of course," Edie said, dropping her gaze to the desk and feeling the heat of a faint blush steal over her cheeks. Why was it that he could apparently reduce her to blushes with simply a glance? "But – I'm not sure how long I'll be here. Perhaps you shouldn't get accustomed to me helping out…"

"I'll use you while I've got you," Curtis said, and yawned. "Goodness, it's nearly ten o'clock. It's been a long day."

"Yes. I heard Louise and Sophia go up to bed a little while ago."

But neither of them made any move to go to their rooms themselves.

"Louise told me a little bit of your story," Curtis said at last. "If you don't want to go back to Boston, I can certainly understand."

"Thank you," she said softly. "It's a difficult decision."

"Don't rush into anything. I know this isn't what you expected – but you're welcome to stay here under my roof as long as you like."

When she looked up at him again, she knew that her hope was shining in her eyes.

"Curtis – I have to ask you. It seems that we've been getting along, after all – and I know that you appreciate my help."

"Certainly," he said, nodding.

"Do you suppose that – well, is it possible that – my words seem to be all jumbled up, I'm sorry. Might Sophia's letter not have been such a tremendous mistake, after all?"

She could not bring herself to put it more plainly than that. But he understood her.

With regret, he shook his head slowly.

"I'm sorry, Edie," he said. "I like you, I do. But I don't plan on getting married again. And I don't reckon that anything will change my mind." He eyed her keenly. "Does that disappoint you?"

Her heart was thumping wildly, her stomach seemed to have sunk to the vicinity of her toes.

"Disappointed isn't the word for it," she said faintly. "But it does answer one question. I cannot stay here with you and Sophia, Curtis – as much as I'd like to." She met his gaze with more courage than she felt. "You see – I like you, too. And if I stay too long…there may need to be another word for that, too."

To his credit, he had the grace to look embarrassed. His gaze dropped away from hers.

"I'm sorry," he said again. "I'm just – stubborn, I guess."

Edie managed a faint smile.

"Well," she said, "that does seem to run in your family. Good night, Curtis."

"Good night, Edie."

She took herself and her disappointment up the stairs and put them both to bed.

CHAPTER 10

Edie awoke the next morning with a firm resolve: she would leave Emerson Ranch, leave Fort Riggins, as soon as she could. Her attraction to Curtis Emerson was growing by the day, and with her hopes of a resolution dashed, she knew only heartbreak would follow if she stayed.

Where would she go? That remained to be seen.

Perhaps she would put in an advertisement, she thought with rather desultory humor.

She could not bring herself to tell Sophia right away. The cheerful girl was positively bouncing that morning as she helped her grandmother with breakfast.

"I forgot about the church," she announced as Edie poured herself some coffee. Edie blinked at her.

"Forgot what about the church?"

"The church needs a new roof. There's going to be a fair next week. That means that Grandma and I are going to bake a lot of pies to take and sell, to help raise money. We told Mr. Thompson that we would, didn't we, Grandma?"

"That's Father Benjamin to you, Sophia."

"I don't know why," said Sophia candidly. "I already have a pa. Say, can I call him Pa Benjamin?"

Louise just shook her head with a sigh. Edie couldn't hold back her laughter, but it faded swiftly as Curtis walked in. He cast a glance around the room, his eyes lighting briefly on Edie. He gave her a smile, which she returned – though not without effort.

"What's all the hubbub?" he asked.

"Your daughter is just being silly, as usual," said Louise.

"Hmm. Nothing new there, then. Don't give her so much coffee, Lou, maybe she'll calm down a little." He pressed a kiss to Sophia's head. "I'm off to the corrals."

"I thought you fixed them already," Sophia said.

"Evidently my handiwork wasn't as handy as I thought. The wiring's come loose on one of the half-rounds."

"Breakfast is almost ready," Louise told him.

"I'll catch something later. Andy's going to train Big Mabel this morning, but he can't do it if the fence is down." He waved at them all and disappeared out the door. Louise shook her head.

"I reckon there's no point in trying to tie that man down," she observed.

Edie sat up straight. "What do you mean by that?"

Louise raised an eyebrow at her sharp tone.

"I mean mealtimes are optional to a working man who runs a ranch," she said mildly. Edie subsided back into her chair, feeling a blush approach from a great distance.

"Oh," she muttered. "I suppose you're right."

There was no doubt about it – she certainly felt odd this morning. The disappointment of Curtis's kind but firm rejection the night before seemed to have grown out of all proportion. On this sunny summer morning, it took the combined efforts of Louise's gentle voice and Sophia's excited enthusiasm to bring Edie back to anything resembling her usual good spirits. Once breakfast was finished and the dishes were cleared, Sophia cast a glance out the window.

"Its beautiful out there," she said, and turned to Edie. "Would you like to take a walk with me?"

Edie glanced at Louise, who smiled at her.

"As long as your grandmother doesn't need us…"

"She doesn't." Sophia took Edie's hand and led her from the kitchen. When Edie cast an apologetic glance over her shoulder, she saw that Louise was chuckling.

"Where are we going?"

"I thought we might walk by the barn," Sophia said. She seemed to be humming with an internal excitement. "I've got something to show you."

"Oh?"

A swift nod. "Can you climb?"

"Why, I'm not sure. I haven't been called on to do much climbing, I confess."

"Of course, you can," Sophia said firmly. "You can do anything, Edie."

The simple faith in her voice was enough to make Edie smile, and she followed the girl up the rickety ladder in the barn to the loft above with scarcely a qualm – provided she didn't look down.

"Goodness. It's warm up here."

"It does get a little hot in the afternoon," Sophia acknowledged. "But I don't mind. I like it up here." She gestured bashfully to the far wall. Around the window placed in the middle, a host of papers were tacked up on the wall. Edie moved closer to look at each one.

"Why – did you do these drawings, Sophia?"

Sophia nodded. It was the first time Edie had ever seen the girl speechless.

Some of the drawings were immediately recognizable – there was Louise, standing at the stovetop with her apron on and a stirring ladle in her hand. There was the ranch house itself, looking cozy and homey with banks of snow covering the landscape around it, only a few branches poking through. There was a sketch of the herd moving past a broken-down fence. There was Curtis, half turned away, his eyes fixed on something only he could see. And there, on paper so new that it hadn't had the chance to fade in the sunlight and heat, was Edie, a smile on her lips as she bent over a ledger on the desk in front of her. There was a simplicity and grace to the drawings that made Edie give a soft sigh. It was obvious the girl had talent; it was equally obvious she also had a deep and affectionate feeling for every subject she had set her hand to.

"These are amazing, Sophia." On impulse, Edie put her arm around the girl and hugged her close. "You're a wonderful artist."

Sophia was blushing brighter than ever.

"Thank you," she murmured. "I like to draw – Grandma gave me some paints for my birthday, and I'm trying my hand at those, too. I'm not very good with them, though."

"Well, I'm certain it's only a matter of time. Practice makes perfect, as they say. How did you get started? How long have you been drawing?"

As Sophia began to open up and tell Edie more about her favorite hobby, the light of the stars came back into her eyes. Edie watched her, smiling. There was something beautiful in seeing someone speak about what they loved – she'd seen a similar expression on Curtis' face when speaking about the ranch. No doubt that same passion had been passed on to his daughter, albeit for a different reason. It made her heart ache – she loved Sophia dearly and hated the thought of leaving her behind. It was almost as painful as the thought of staying here when Curtis had said he was not interested in marriage…

Either way, it seemed an impossible situation. She'd been in impossible situations before – not that long ago, in fact, she thought with the memory of her father and Burton Crowell running through her mind – but she wasn't at all certain how she was going to handle this one.

"How does your father feel about your drawing?"

Sophia hesitated.

"Well," she said slowly, "I don't reckon he knows about it."

"What? Surely not."

"He's just always out working, you see – and I don't think he realizes that I spend so much time up here. I guess I've talked to him about it before, years ago when I was a little girl. But we don't talk too much anymore – about anything." She was quiet for a moment. "He's been different since you got here."

"Do you think so?"

Sophia nodded. "Coming in for meals, sitting with us in the evening – he hardly ever does that kind of thing anymore. It's only since you've been here. I think he likes you, Edie."

Edie sighed. In her mind, the evening previous flashed with a stark and vivid light.

"I'm not sure about that," she said.

"Do you like him?"

She met the girl's gaze. There was no little white lie that could be told her, no side-stepping the issue. Sophia wanted to know – and perhaps, after all, she had a right to.

"Yes," Edie said softly. "I do. I like him very much. Almost as much as you like drawing – tell me, when is the best time for good light?"

The blatant attempt at changing the subject worked – though, Edie suspected, it only worked because Sophia allowed herself to be distracted back into her favorite topic. At last, the conversation quieted down, and Edie noted that Sophia was casting more and more longing glances to the stack of paper and pens on the little desk in the corner. Smiling, she excused herself and made her way back down the ladder, leaving the girl to get back to her drawings.

She couldn't help the broad smile on her lips as she strode out of the barn, any more than she could help the feeling of happiness that soared within her at the warmth of the golden sunlight. She stopped for a moment and breathed deeply, looking about her. The ranch was peaceful and quiet, only the far-off sounds of the mooing herd interrupting the silence. Everything was neat, tidy – cared for. Everywhere she looked there was evidence that Curtis Emerson loved this ranch as much as his daughter loved her drawing – as much as Louise loved her little family. Everyone had something they cared about. Everyone had something they wanted to protect.

She couldn't help but envy them – but even that feeling of longing to belong could not destroy her surge of well-being. Sophia had shown her what mattered most to her, as Louise had said she might. It was a clear expression of the girl's affection for her, and it touched her to the heart.

She was still smiling over the very thought when someone cleared their throat.

Edie nearly jumped, her gaze flying over to him.

"Goodness. You startled me."

Curtis grinned at her.

"So I see, from the way you're clutching at your throat. I'm sorry. I didn't mean to."

"You might try warning a girl before you sneak up on her," Edie chided him, dropping her hand and folding her arms instead. She gave him a teasing smile, still feeling quite overcome by her feeling of happiness. It was gratifying to see him give her a teasing smile in return.

"If I warned you, I wouldn't be able to sneak up. Besides, I was standing here already when you came out of the barn." He moved toward her. "If anything, you're the one who snuck up on me."

"You were standing there?" She raised her eyebrows. "I didn't see you. You must have been very quiet."

"I was," he acknowledged. "I was eavesdropping, you see – but don't tell my daughter, because that's precisely what I've always told her not to do."

Edie laughed at his frankness. "Eavesdropping on what?"

"You mean on who."

"On..." She stopped and tilted her head to one side curiously. "On Sophia and me? In the attic."

"It's called a hayloft," he said, taking another step toward her. "As you seem to have found out, it's where the hay is kept."

In response to her look of puzzlement, he reached out and took a piece of straw from among the loosened locks of her hair.

"Oh," she said, with a breathless little laugh, and took it from him. "I didn't even realize…"

He was standing quite close to her now, looking down at her with an expression that she couldn't quite read – but which she rather liked. A feeling of excitement began to bubble up from somewhere around her toes, working its way upward.

"I heard how you two talked together," he said. "Sophia really likes you, you know."

"Do you think so?"

"Mm-hmm." He shrugged one shoulder. "But that isn't really the word for it, is it? I think she loves you."

She smiled.

"I love her, too," she said. "I was just thinking about that – about how difficult it's going to be to say goodbye."

Curtis took in a deep breath.

"Suppose you didn't have to."

Edie stared up at him, and he winked one dark eye, smiling.

"But I must," she said. "I told you last night – I don't think I can cope with staying here when you...when you're not interested in marriage, generally speaking." She peered at him. "And you're not – interested in marriage, are you?"

Curtis folded his arms. "That's right," he said. "I'm not."

The feeling of excitement began to simmer down once more, replaced by the same disappointment she had felt the evening before.

"Well, then," she said helplessly, "what on earth do you propose we do?"

He grinned at her, a bright, brief grin, and then took her face in his hands and kissed her. It was a gentle kiss, but she felt as though she were melting into him, and when he let her go, she realized her arms had found their way around his neck. She gazed at him, wide-eyed.

"Curtis Emerson," she said. "One or both of us is very confused."

"I know who my money's on," said Curtis, and laughed. "I meant what I said, Edie Kendall – I'm not interested in marriage, generally speaking. But marrying you, on the other hand – despite myself, I find that interesting. You might almost say...intriguing. I think that might be the word." He kissed her again, and she pushed him away and took a step back. Her head was spinning.

"Please explain precisely what you mean," she said, "before you do that again. If I find out you're toying with my feelings…"

"I wouldn't," said Curtis, and there was a blunt honesty in his words that she recognized. "I'd never. I couldn't. Listen, Edie, from the moment I first saw you I was…drawn to you. I certainly didn't want to be. What Sophia did was downright foolish, and she had no right to try and arrange a new wife for me. I was doing just fine on my own – at least, that's what I thought."

He shook his head. "I reckon it's a case of not knowing what I was missing until it was right there under my nose." He sighed. "I missed Ruth – I reckon I always will. She was a special person – and she loved me dearly, far more dearly than I had any right to be loved. She wouldn't have wanted me to be unhappy – and she sure wouldn't have wanted me to make our daughter unhappy. There I was, pushing away anything that might have fixed it all – pushing away the very suggestion of moving on. And then you showed up, and I pushed you away, too."

His dark eyes met hers once more. "I promised Sophia that I'd try – and I should have known then and there she'd win in the end. She always said she knew what was best for me. Maybe she does."

Edie took his hands in hers.

"She loves you, you know," she said. "That's all it comes down to. She loves you, and she was afraid of losing you."

"I know," Curtis said. "I don't know how I ever came to deserve to be loved by her – or liked by you." Another grin, and Edie felt her knees wobble. "But when she decided to show you her drawings, and I heard you two talking in the hayloft, well – I knew I couldn't hold out any longer. Stubborn as I am, I have to give in."

They held hands tightly.

"Well, Curtis Emerson," she said. "I'd still like a little more explanation as to what, precisely, you intend. I don't suppose you like me after all, do you?" she asked him teasingly. He met her gaze with his, his eyes deep and unfathomable – but with a spark of warmth somewhere down below.

"Like doesn't begin to cover it," he said. "I reckon there's another word for it."

"Oh, yes?"

He grinned.

"And I reckon you know what it is, too."

This time, when he kissed her, she was ready for it.

There came a brief shriek from the hayloft window, far above them, and they stepped apart, both of them laughing – and both of them blushing.

"Reckon we got caught," said Curtis.

Edie put her arms around him.

"Reckon it won't be the last time," she said, and she held him tight.

The End

CONTINUE READING...

Thank you for reading *Sophia's New Mother!* Are you wondering **what to read next?** Why not read *The Sheriff's New Bride?* **Here's a peek for you:**

It was a cold autumn morning in Spring Valley, Texas, and there was blood on the wind.

Scott Bailey, sitting in the sheriff's office with his head in his hands and poring over a dispatch from the Clarion County courthouse, sat up straight. A seven-year veteran of serving the law, he'd developed a sort of sixth sense to tell him when trouble was about to crop up. It was alerting him now. As quiet as the chilly morning was, that peace was about to be shattered – he just didn't know how.

Seated at the desk across from him, his deputy glanced up, putting his pencil down.

"What's up, Scott?"

Sheriff Bailey narrowed his eyes, turning to the window. "Thought I heard something."

A silence fell over the two men, thick as a blanket.

"I don't hear a thing," John Miller started, but there was a call from the distance, faint but clear nonetheless, just as he began to speak. Scott was up from his chair and headed to the door before John even finished his sentence.

He pulled open the heavy wooden door to the jailhouse and stepped out onto the split-wood sidewalk, looking up and down the street.

"Mr. Calloway? What do you hear?"

"Sounds like someone's shouting for you, Sheriff."

Scott glanced over his shoulder at his deputy, but John Miller was already on his feet, reaching for his coat.

Ahead of the tumult, the word spread from person to person, as each came within hearing range and passed on the message.

"It's Cody Brown."

"He's on foot – he can't have run all the way from the ranch."

"He must have, look at how the poor boy is out of breath."

"Where's the sheriff? Cody's asking for him."

But Scott was tightening the saddle on his horse, listening to the words spilling here and there around him. By the time Cody Brown came into view, the sheriff was already on horseback. He nudged Gallant with his heels and the big black horse moved forward obediently a few steps.

"What is it, Cody?"

Visit HERE To Read More!

https://ticahousepublishing.com/mail-order-brides.html

THANKS FOR READING!

If you **love Mail Order Bride Romance**, **Visit Here**

https://wesrom.subscribemenow.com/

to find out about all **New Susannah Calloway Romance Releases! We will let you know as soon as they become available!**

If you enjoyed *Sophia's New Mother,* would you kindly take a couple minutes to leave a positive review on Amazon? It only takes a moment, and positive reviews truly make a difference. Thank you so much! I appreciate it!

Turn the page to discover more Mail Order Bride Romances just for you!

MORE MAIL ORDER BRIDE ROMANCES FOR YOU!

We love clean, sweet, adventurous Mail Order Bride Romances and have a lovely library of Susannah Calloway titles just for you!

Box Sets — A Wonderful Bargain for You!

https://ticahousepublishing.com/bargains-mob-box-sets.html

Or enjoy Susannah's single titles. You're sure to find many favorites! (Remember all of them can be downloaded FREE with Kindle Unlimited!)

Sweet Mail Order Bride Romances!

https://ticahousepublishing.com/mail-order-brides.html

ABOUT THE AUTHOR

Susannah has always been intrigued with the Western movement - prairie days, mail-order brides, the gold rush, frontier life! As a writer, she's excited to combine her love of story with her love of all that is Western. Presently, Susannah lives in Wyoming with her hubby and their three amazing children.

www.ticahousepublishing.com
contact@ticahousepublishing.com

f

Made in the USA
Middletown, DE
03 November 2022

14065197R00056